I0624768

HELL'S SERPENT

MICHAEL YOWELL

SEVEREDPRESS

www.facebook.com/MichaelYowell

michaelyowellhorror@gmail.com

ISBN: 978-1-923165-64-9

PREFACE

One of the things I loved the most growing up as a boy was watching campy horror movies on TV every Saturday at noon. Especially the giant-creature movies from the '50s and '60s, like *Them!*, *Tarantula*, *The Deadly Mantis*, *It Came From Beneath The Sea*, *Godzilla*, and *The War Of The Gargantuas*. They helped to warp my mind. In fact, if it weren't for them, I might never have started writing horror stories.

So. Imagine you're back in your youth, it's a rainy Saturday afternoon, and you're sitting on the couch or your favorite chair. You switch the TV to that beloved channel and begin to lose yourself watching this tale....

CHAPTER 1

OKLAHOMA, 1960

Miles beneath the shale and limestone, the creature stirred.

It was woken again by lengthy sets of vibrations in the earth, interrupting its underground slumber. Its extraordinary senses could feel the vibrations carry through the rock. It could also hear distant sounds. It heard muffled concussions and the slightest strikes of objects upon rock.

The sounds and vibrations beckoned its response. The creature slowly started to move, using the muscles attached to its rib bones to crawl forward. It continued to receive occasional series of vibrations. This spurred and excited the creature, while at the same time irritated and angered it.

It rose higher through its network of tunnels to find the source.

CHAPTER 2

"Tom Defray, I swear… you're incorrigible."

The determined college student set his blue eyes upon Betty Lou and grinned. "Who, me?"

"Yes, you," Betty Lou Wiggins said, still grasping his hand that she had removed from her cheek. "You need to be patient."

Tom nodded obediently. "I'm sorry, Betty Lou. It's just that you're so darn pretty that I *have* to kiss you."

She giggled. She knew her boyfriend well enough to know that he would say anything to weaken her defenses. But she also knew that the sweet geology student was genuinely taken by her and would do anything she wished. She dissuaded him.

"Later, dear," she said. "Now let's just get on with our studying. We only have thirty minutes until the final."

"You're right." Tom regained focus of his studies. This was the week of final exams, and they were about to take their last of the semester. After that, summer vacation could begin.

***

The exam went very well for Tom and Betty Lou. Thanks to them cramming their brains beforehand, each of them was able to provide almost every right answer. The exam would surely seal their good grades in that course and make their respective parents proud.

The students filtered out of the building and walked across the campus to the parking lot. Tom and Betty Lou held hands while heading for Tom's green Jeep.

Waiting there was his best friend, Chad Burton. A smile emerged on Chad's darkly-tanned face when he saw the couple approach.

"It's about time," he said. "I've been waiting impatiently."

"So, you're stoked about our camping trip?"

"Damn right I am!" Chad said excitedly. "It's gonna be a blast!"

Tom nodded. "That it is." The three longtime friends had planned to spend the weekend camping at their favorite secluded spot atop the hills north of Little Mountain State Park.

The trio got into the Jeep. Chad jumped into the back seat with his backpack, and Betty Lou buckled up in the passenger seat. Tom turned the key and started the engine.

Tom leaned into his girlfriend. "How about a kiss for the road?"

"Later, dear," she said, her head retreating.

Tom chuckled. Betty Lou was a proper enough girl, all right; kissing in public was not appropriate to her.

"All right, Romeo," said Chad. "Let's go, already."

Tom pulled away from the parking lot and drove along Main Street. Glancing down at the gas gauge, he noticed they were almost on E.

"I've got to get gas before we go camping." Tom looked for Mr. Glover's Texaco station, spotting it coming up on the right. He turned in.

Pulling into the gas station, they saw three young men together in the garage. There was the town bully, Robbie Sullivan, and his greaser pals, Tony and Jeff, all of whom worked there. They didn't seem to be working very hard, though; they were swilling bottles of beer while chatting in their coveralls.

Tom parked next to the pumps, and the employees wandered out to meet them. All three of them had their hair slicked back the same way.

"Fill 'er up, please," said Tom. "We're going camping this weekend, so I need a full tank."

Robbie approached the college kids. He looked at Tom with disdain; he had disliked the brainy wimp ever since elementary school. Robbie hated how Tom looked particularly smug today in his red-and-white plaid button-up shirt. He hated him even more because Tom had Betty Lou.

"Camping, huh?" Robbie scoffed. "What kind of panty-waist goes camping?"

His cohorts snickered behind him.

Betty Lou squeezed Tom's leg anxiously. She did not want a confrontation.

Tom ignored his adrenaline. "Never mind, Robbie, I'll do it myself." He stepped out of the Jeep and reached for the nozzle.

Robbie pushed his hand away. "I don't think so, Tom."

Tom noticed a fresh cigarette burn on Robbie's arm. *Probably another "gift" from his alcoholic father*, Tom figured.

Chad and Betty Lou got out of the Jeep and stood beside Tom. "Say, what's wrong with you?" said Chad.

"Nothin', pal," Robbie said, snarling his lip at the lanky man. "What's wrong with *you*? You want a knuckle sandwich?"

Betty Lou tried to calm them down. "All right, fellas, we don't want any trouble. We just want some gas."

Robbie took her in with his eyes. She looked sexy in that tight-fitting sleeveless tunic, its geometric pattern drawing him in. He had always desired Betty Lou, ever since middle school. She had the most beautiful hazel eyes and long, wavy brown hair. She'd grown a terrific figure as well. But they were from opposite sides of the tracks.

"What are you doin' with *that* flake when you could be with a real man?" said Robbie.

"Because," Betty Lou replied, "unlike you, he *is* a real man." She then planted her lips on her boyfriend's, giving him a long, passionate kiss.

Robbie scowled. *That bitch*, he thought. His blood began to boil.

When the kiss was over, Tom turned his head to Robbie. "Did you hear that?" he beamed. "A real man."

"I'll show you how a man should kiss," said Robbie, gripping Betty Lou by the arms.

Tom stiffened. "Hey!"

Robbie's eyes turned hard. "What are you gonna do about it?" he goaded, ready for action.

Tom did not want to fight the tough young man. But he had to do something to come to Betty Lou's aid. Even if it meant getting into a fistfight.

He stepped forward.

Chad decided to quickly intervene. "Maybe I should just tell my father about you all drinking while at work."

Robbie's heart jumped. Chad was the son of Sheriff Burton, and Robbie knew so. He thought twice; there was no way he wanted to invite a visit from the police.

"All right, all right," Robbie complied. He released his grip and let Betty Lou go. "There's no need to bother with the sheriff. No need for tattling." He backed up to give everyone some space.

Tom eased down. "C'mon, guys," he said to his friends, "we'll stop somewhere else for gas." He watched while Betty Lou and Chad took their seats in the Jeep. Then he hopped into the driver seat and started the vehicle. Tom kept his eye on Robbie while he pulled away.

"But don't think this is the end of it," Robbie blurted as they left. "This isn't over!"

Not by a long shot, he seethed.

Tom steered through town, heading for the next gas station. His pulse was still brisk from the confrontation.

"Can you believe that guy?" said Chad, shaking his head.

"Yeah," Tom said, "I can. He's always been that way. Bad news."

"You said it."

Tom glanced over at Betty Lou. "Thanks for the kiss," he said. "But what happened to 'later, dear'?"

"That *was* later," she replied, and everyone in the vehicle shared a laugh.

***

After dropping off Chad and Betty Lou at their houses so they could pack for the weekend, Tom drove home to do his own packing. He pulled into the driveway and trotted to the front door.

Hank Defray, his father, took note of Tom's arrival. "That you, son?"

"Yeah, Dad," said Tom, entering the living room.

"How was your last final?"

"Oh, it was really good. Easier than I thought it would be. I'll get an A for sure."

"Great! Your mother would be so proud of you." Hank reached for his pipe and stuffed it with his favorite tobacco. He lit it and puffed on it.

Tom never understood the appeal of smoking a pipe. It seemed like something stuffy people or old people did. But he didn't mind; the tobacco his father smoked left a pleasant scent of cherry.

"Uh oh," Hank noticed, "looks like Elsa got out of her tank again."

Tom scanned the room and saw the pet boa constrictor stretched out on the back of the sofa. "Oh, Elsa," he said, walking over to her. "Do we need to put a latch on your cover?" He picked up the snake and cradled her in his arms. "She doesn't even resist," Tom remarked.

"Typical behavior from a Peruvian boa," said Hank, who knew what he was talking about. He was a herpetologist, which made him well versed in reptiles and amphibians. "Those long-tails are one of the calmest of the species."

Tom placed the boa inside her glass tank, and then replaced the metal screened cover. "Now stay in there, Elsa."

"Ready for your camping trip?" Hank asked.

"Just about. I've got to pack my backpack. But I already have the tent and sleeping bag out and ready to go."

"Don't forget the lanterns. And matches for the kerosene."

"I won't."

"And the flashlight."

"I've got it."

Hank casually blew a smoke ring. "And don't forget to bring an extra jacket. Just in case."

"Dad," Tom chuckled, appreciating his father's overprotectiveness, "don't worry. I'm gonna be just fine up there."

CHAPTER 3

Tom honked the horn. A moment later, Chad exited the house and lugged his gear to the Jeep. He tucked his sleeping bag, tent, and fishing pole in the back, then climbed into the back seat.

"All right, here we go!" said Chad.

Tom nodded. "We already got gas and beer—"

"—And food," Betty Lou added.

"And food. All that's left to do is get up there."

"Then what are you waiting for, Daddy-O? Step on it!"

Tom put the Jeep into gear and drove off, getting back to Main Street. Taking it north, he got out of town and onto the two-lane highway that led to the state park.

After a short while, they came up on Frannie's Diner, their favorite weekly hangout. Tom honked the horn and gave a ceremonial wave to any classmates who might be glancing out through the hazy windows. He continued driving up the highway and into the heavier woods.

Betty Lou, smiling in the warm breeze, was utterly happy in the passenger seat. Tilting her head, she said, "I can't wait to take a dip in the lake. Finals had me super stressed out!"

Tom nodded, his short, blond hair bristling in the wind. "You're not kidding; this year was rough. I'm ready to set up my tent, start a fire, and drink a cold one!"

"Don't forget the fishing," added Chad, leaning forward from the back seat. "I'm gonna catch us the biggest dinner we've ever had!" His boastful grin was wide.

"We'll see," taunted Betty Lou, pulling her hair away from her eyes. "I'm still waiting to see you bring in the big one!"

Tom chuckled in agreement; his friend never had much success fishing. The three continued ribbing each other while Tom pressed the accelerator to get to their destination sooner.

Tom had taken this route many times since he and his campus buddies had found the remote location years before. The highway led right to Little Mountain State Park, which would likely be crowded this weekend. Luckily, he and his friends were instead going to pass the park and turn off onto a road that led to another trailhead.

At the end of the dirt road, Tom parked the Jeep and shut off the engine. "We're here!" he announced unnecessarily.

The drive was over; now it was just a one-mile hike to the most beautiful and secluded place they could hope to be in. Then they would set up camp and begin to properly celebrate their freedom from this semester's studies.

They unloaded the gear from the back and organized it. Once they figured out how they were carrying the sleeping bags, tents, backpacks, and rolling cooler, the three began their trek up the wooded trail.

***

They navigated the familiar rocky path for half an hour, through oaks and elms, until they reached the top of the plateau that led to their campers' paradise. Tom felt the relief of arrival wash over him. "Here we are," he announced, "just over this slope."

To their surprise, however, the area looked nothing like how they remembered it.

Tom's jaw dropped. "What in the world…?"

The group found themselves standing at the edge of a cliff that had never been there before. What used to be a level plane, complete with freshwater streams feeding into a small, unruffled lake, was now gone. Now the area looked like a gigantic crater. It was as if the plateau's entire foundation sank, dropping everything a hundred feet.

"What's this?" exclaimed Chad, involuntarily keeping hold of Betty Lou's thin arm. "What the hell happened up here?"

"I don't know," Tom replied after a moment of contemplation. "Was there an earthquake?"

"Couldn't be," offered Betty Lou, "or we would've felt it in town."

"You know," said Chad, with a cocked eyebrow, "they *have* been doing a lot of drilling near this area lately. I wonder if that had anything to do with the stability of the ground here."

Tom surveyed the land below. For the most part, the area looked intact. Despite having fallen, the ground was solid down there. Most of the trees were still rooted and standing strong, and the streams had found their way down the new walls and eventually into what was left of their familiar lake. Whatever happened changed the landscape dramatically, but did not seem to destroy it.

"That couldn't cause this," Tom presumed. "Drilling affects individual areas. What we have here is an unbelievable amount of earth vanishing beneath the ground. About three hundred yards across, I'd say. It's... amazing."

"What could cause that?" asked Betty Lou.

"I don't know."

"Come on, you're the geology major," Chad charged.

Tom's eyes met Chad's. "Are you kidding? We've never read about anything like *this* in our textbooks!"

Chad nodded. "I'll give you that."

"Maybe," Tom hypothesized, "it was some giant sinkhole that did it." He shrugged. "Let's find a way down there. I wanna check it out up close."

Chad was dumbfounded. "What? You just said *sinkhole!* That doesn't sound safe to me."

"It seems to be settled now," said Tom. "Everything looks stabilized. Even the streams flowing into the lake. I'm sure it's fine down there. Come on, let's go."

"Down this cliff?" Betty Lou protested. "With all our gear?"

"Yeah, sure," smiled Tom. "C'mon, there's got to be an easier way down somewhere around here."

Reluctantly, the other two followed their ambitious friend along the rim of the new crater to look for a good way down. Within minutes, they found an area where earth and rock had slid to the bottom to create a navigable slope.

"This looks good," said Tom. He took hold of Betty Lou's arm and started down the ramp of loose dirt, mindful not to lose his footing. Chad followed in Tom's footsteps.

"Wow," said Chad when they reached the bottom. "It looks about the same as it used to. See? Those are the trees we usually follow to get to the creek."

Betty Lou followed Chad's finger, noting that he was right. The entire area was still very familiar despite having fallen a hundred feet down. The small lake had suffered the most change, but even it was mostly intact; there just wasn't as much water in it as there used to be. Her eyes continued scanning the scenery within the cliff walls, and something disturbing caught her eye.

There was a large opening in the craggy rock; a hole about twenty feet wide and fifteen feet high. And in the instant her eyes passed it, she thought she saw something large moving in the shadows of the cave. She gasped.

"What is it?" Tom asked. "What's the matter?"

Betty Lou looked again, harder.

Nothing was moving in the cave.

"Nothing," she finally admitted. "I thought I saw something in that cave there."

The men drew their eyes to the hole in the cliff and looked for themselves.

"My eyes were just playing tricks on me," said Betty Lou, "...I hope."

"Don't worry," assured Chad. "Until recently, that cave didn't exist; not above ground, anyway. I don't think any animals would've made it their home this quickly."

Tom draped his arm around the object of his desire. "C'mon, Betty Lou. Let's get camp set up so we can have some fun." Giving one last glance to the gaping hole in the rock wall, Betty Lou nodded.

"You're sure it's safe to camp down here?" Chad said cautiously.

"Yeah, buddy. Don't worry. Look, if we hear or feel any ground start to move, we'll make a run for the perimeter. Okay?"

Chad felt satisfied with that reasoning. "Okay."

The three journeyed toward what was left of the lake in the middle of the crater. They found their usual site, not far from the edge of the small lake. Then they happily relieved themselves of their gear and began to set up the tents.

***

By sunset, Tom had a campfire going strong. And true to his reputation, Chad had returned to the campsite without any fish. Fortunately, Betty Lou had brought some fried chicken that her mother made for them.

"I wish your mom had made more than this," Chad commented.

Betty Lou grinned. "Well, as far as my parents know, it's just me and Melanie camping this weekend."

"Yeah, she has no idea you're with two hungry men," said Tom. "At least she's known us for a long time."

"And she likes you both," added Betty Lou. "But that doesn't mean she'd approve of me going camping with boys."

"Your secret's safe with us," Tom said playfully.

After they ate, they positioned themselves around the fire. They talked about various subjects while digesting their dinner.

The sun's light was soon gone from the sky, and the stars began to show overhead. The three contented students sipped beers and relaxed under the clear night sky.

CHAPTER 4

The following morning, Tom woke to a pleasant sound. His ears detected the trickling of the nearby stream and the songs of birds. He unzipped his sleeping bag, sat up, and stretched his arms.

Betty Lou heard the movement and she stirred. Rolling over and opening her eyes, she saw her boyfriend smiling at her.

"Good morning," he said. "How did you sleep?"

"Fine," she said timidly.

Tom leaned toward her and kissed her forehead. "Good. Me too." Still in his sweatpants, he crawled over to his shoes and put them on. Then he unzipped the tent and went outside to relieve his bladder.

Betty Lou opened her sleeping bag and got out. Making sure she looked presentable enough, she emerged from the tent and walked to the smoldering remains of the campfire.

"We need to find more wood," she muttered to herself.

Looking around, she saw Chad wandering in the

distance. He had apparently been thinking the same thought; he already had his arms full of dry tree limbs.

"Oh good," she said. She then went to her cooler to dig for her small skillet and container of eggs.

Tom returned from behind a tree, feeling much better. He went to Betty Lou's side. "Whatcha doing?" he said.

"Preparing breakfast," she replied.

"What are we having?"

"Nothing fancy. Just some scrambled eggs and toast."

"Sounds great," said Tom, his stomach awakened by the mention of food. "Can I help?"

She shooed him away. "No, dear, it's a one-person job. You'd just be in the way."

That was fine with him. "All right." He turned his head to Chad. "Morning, Chad."

"Morning." Chad dumped his pile of wood next to the campfire. "I got more wood for tonight."

"You mean this morning," Betty Lou smiled. "We need a fire to cook breakfast."

"Okay," said Chad. He stirred up some of the embers and caught fire to some kindling. Then he topped that with two fatter pieces of wood. A fire was quickly going.

Betty Lou mixed some eggs in the skillet and scrambled them over the heat of the fire. It didn't take long to cook them. She served them onto three paper plates, and then she laid bread in the heated skillet to toast it.

It wasn't a gourmet meal by any means, but it did satiate their hunger and fuel them for the start of their day. When they were finished eating, Tom thanked her and tossed his paper plate into the fire.

"What shall we do today?" Chad wondered. "Wanna try some fishing?"

"Sure," said Tom. "I'll take a turn."

"That's if there are still fish in there after what happened here," Betty remarked.

"I'm sure there are," Tom asserted. "The entire plate of the area collapsed at the same time, so there's no place the fish could've been lost to."

"I'm certainly gonna keep trying to catch some," said Chad.

"You're coming to the lake too, aren't you?" Tom asked Betty Lou.

"I might wade in the water a little," she declared. After all, they had all packed their swimsuits in anticipation of going for a dip.

"Now, what do you think the best lure would be to catch a trout?" said Chad. "I forgot to bring salmon eggs, but I do have some spinning lures."

"I wonder if there might be something around here that we could use as bait," Tom pondered.

"Like what?"

"I dunno. Maybe grubs or worms. Or even berries."

"Or crickets, or grasshoppers," Betty Lou added.

"Good idea," said Chad. "Let's take a walk and look around."

The trio searched the ground and around bushes and trees. Chad tripped on a protruding tree root hidden by weeds, and he almost fell over. He caught his balance by stretching his other leg to stop his fall.

"Watch your step," Tom giggled.

Chad was cool about it. He simply replied, "I did."

They continued searching their surroundings. They used sticks to dig into the earth, hoping to uncover something alive. But they found no bait.

Chad turned his head toward an area covered in tall switchgrass.

"Maybe there are grasshoppers over there in the grassier area," he mused. He headed that way, and his friends followed.

While they walked in that direction, Betty Lou gazed up at the cave in the cliffside and studied it. She recalled her eyes playing tricks on her yesterday by making her think she had seen something large moving inside the darkness. She paused for a better look.

"What's the matter?" asked Tom.

"Nothing," she replied. "Just looking at that cave."

"We should check it out," said Chad. "It might be really cool inside. Maybe we'll even find some gold or silver in there!"

Tom winced skeptically. "What?"

"Seriously! After all, nobody's seen this part of the underground except for us. And they're drilling all around here."

"So?"

"So? What do you think they're looking for?"

"Oil or gas, I'd bet," said Tom.

Chad rolled his eyes. "Sure, maybe. But that doesn't mean there isn't gold or silver in the ground."

Tom chuckled. "All right, pal. Let's go check it out."

The trio crossed the plane and arrived at the side of the crater. The freshly-exposed face of rock and earth was steep, but the group saw a manageable route up the hillside to the opening. They climbed about twenty feet, and then they were standing at the mouth of the cave.

"This is one enormous cave," Tom commented, his eyes looking all around the oval-shaped tunnel. The sunlight that wandered in reflected on the rough surfaces of the expanse.

"What do you think made this?" said Betty Lou.

"Usually caves are caused by the erosion of bedrock such as limestone," Tom replied, "but I can't imagine anything like that being substantial enough to create *this*."

"Come on," said Chad, "let's go inside."

They walked slowly into the dark cave. The farther they went, the less residual light from the opening was present to aid their eyes. They were about a hundred feet in when a strong scent struck their noses.

"What is that smell?" Betty Lou wondered.

"Dunno," said Chad. "It doesn't smell like dirt or rock; it's a different kind of musty."

"Yeah," Tom said, "it definitely doesn't have that earthy scent."

"Natural gas, maybe?"

Tom shook his head. "No, not that."

"What, then?"

"It smells more like… a pachyderm."

Betty Lou's eyebrows rose. "A what?"

"Pachyderm. You know, like an elephant or a rhinoceros. Remember what they smelled like at the zoo?"

She could place the scent now. "You're right. It's a lot like that. But still a little different."

"Well, if it's not dirt, rock, or natural gas," said Chad, "then it might be some kind of animal smell. And that means we should scram."

Tom concurred. "Yeah, you're right. This might not be the safest place for us to be."

"Probably not," said Betty Lou, agreeing completely. "Let's get out of here."

They turned and walked back to the entrance, daylight guiding them.

Behind them, in the darkness, something moved quietly. It had smelled the strange beings and become agitated. The scent was interpreted as both adversary and prey. The creature wanted to pursue and kill, but the skin beneath its translucent scales was too sensitive to the light ahead. It would have to wait.

It would hunt tonight.

CHAPTER 5

"I'm bored." Robbie Sullivan took a drag on his cigarette. He blew out the smoke, then spat on the pavement.

"Wanna get some burgers?" said Tony.

Robbie looked at him, contemplating. "Sure," he decided. They had eaten not long ago, but it was after noon, and Robbie was always hungry. "Let's go."

He led his pals to his blue Chevy Biscayne, and they piled in. Robbie started the car and drove toward Main Street.

"Maybe we'll pick up some chicks there," Tony hoped, watching pedestrians as they drove by.

"Yeah," Jeff responded. "Maybe we can bring 'em back to our place."

Robbie doubted that. Their usual scores were drunken women whom they had befriended after hours at a bar or a party behind the chat piles. Those women paid no mind to the condition of the rundown house

Tony and Jeff were renting. But it would be quite different for sober girls in the middle of the day.

"Maybe," said Robbie, just to keep their hopes alive.

They pulled into the parking lot of the Ku-Ku Burger. The young men jumped out of the car, tucked their tight shirts into their weathered jeans, and walked inside the restaurant.

They sat down in a booth along a brick partition and chatted until they were greeted by the familiar waitress, Beth. They placed their orders, said some bold things to the waitress, and watched her shake her head and walk away. It was a game; Beth knew the guys well enough to play along with them just enough to get a reaction from them.

Beth brought their food out and laid it out before them. Then, while smacking her gum, she told them to enjoy their food and strutted away. The guys dug into their cheeseburgers and fries.

While they ate, Jeff glanced around the restaurant. He saw a variety of townspeople that were familiar to him, but not any young women that he and his pals could hit on. Then, in a corner, he saw the local herpetologist Hank Defray, quietly sipping coffee and reading the newspaper.

"There's Tom Defray's old man," said Jeff, and the others looked over.

"He's some sort of scientist, isn't he?" Tony asked.

"Yeah. Works with snakes or something creepy like that."

"Look at that putz," Robbie snarled. "Just like his loser son."

Jeff turned to Robbie. "That loser son got his hands on Betty Lou Wiggins," he jeered.

"Betty Lou Wiggins," Robbie echoed. "That mirror warmer is too stuck up. He can have her. She's his baggage."

Tony and Jeff were not fooled; they knew Robbie had always wanted Betty Lou. They deemed it best, however, not to call him out on it. They kept their mouths shut and kept eating.

After a few more bites, Robbie spoke up. "That Tom's got a lot of nerve. The way he looked at me with that stupid smile. I should punch his lights out."

"Good thing you didn't," said Jeff. "His pal's old man is the sheriff, you know."

"I know. That's the only thing that saved him yesterday." Robbie replayed the events in his mind. Seeing Betty Lou give Tom that big kiss infuriated him.

"Let's go find that putz," Robbie proposed, his voice resolute.

The others grinned. "Yeah?" said Jeff.

"Yeah," said Robbie. "Gonna teach him a painful lesson."

"What if his friend Chad is with him?"

"Then we teach them *both* a lesson."

"But the sheriff—" Tony began.

"Screw the sheriff," Robbie snarled. "Those guys need to know who's boss in this town. Even if it means they… go missing."

Jeff snickered and nodded in agreement.

"Didn't they say they were going camping this weekend?" said Tony.

"That's right," Robbie replied, recalling what Tom had said at the gas station. "They did. We should go find them while they're out there. Then there'd be no witnesses to tell the sheriff anything."

"Yeah."

A cruel grin curled up Robbie's lip. "And I'm gonna show that Betty Lou what a real man can do."

***

Robbie's blue Biscayne rolled through the parking lot at Little Mountain State Park. They looked around, seeing an assortment of cars in the parking spaces. To their disappointment, however, the Jeep belonging to Tom Defray was nowhere to be seen.

"They're not camping here," said Robbie. "Where the hell could they be?"

"I dunno," Jeff mumbled. "Are there any other campgrounds around?"

Robbie shook his head. "Not that I know about. Maybe they just made camp in some random spot in the woods." He sped up, taking them out of the parking lot. "Let's keep driving," he said, "and maybe we'll spot his car farther up the road."

He drove them back to the two-lane highway and continued north. It did not take long for them to see the dirt road leading off to the right.

"What's this?" Robbie muttered. "Let's check it out."

He slowed down and turned onto the dirt road. He followed it for about half a mile until it ended at a trailhead. And there, parked on the side, was Tom's Jeep.

"Ha!" said Robbie. "We got 'em."

He pulled up alongside the Jeep and turned the engine off. Then he and his boys hopped out of the car and looked around the surrounding trees.

"Which way do you think they went?" asked Jeff.

"No idea," Robbie said. "But we'll find them up there somewhere." His eyes continued scanning the woods. "It looks like there's a little trail over there. Come on."

Tony pulled out his switchblade knife. "Let's slash his tires first."

"No, don't!" Robbie blurted.

"What? Why not?"

"I don't want any proof left that we were here."

Confused, they looked at him in disbelief.

"Just in case," Robbie said, "things go south up there."

The others knew what he meant. In the event that they killed someone, they would have to scram and claim that they were someplace else at the time if questioned.

"Now let's go find 'em," said Robbie, and the others followed him onto the trail and up the hillside.

***

They hiked for half an hour, weaving through the oaks and elms. By then, the top of the hill was visible.

"We're at the top," Robbie said quietly. "Still don't see 'em, though."

"Maybe they're just over the hill," whispered Tony.

"Okay. Keep going."

The three men reached the top and looked down in awe. They had not expected to see a vast crater on the plateau. It looked like the opening of a volcano. But unlike a volcano, the crater hosted plant life, streams, and a lake. It was fascinating.

"Look! Look!" said Jeff, pointing to the center of the crater. "It's a tent!"

"Two, it looks like," Robbie acknowledged. He looked hard, and he could make out the faces of the three people down there. Sure enough, they had found their victims.

"How do we get down there?" wondered Jeff.

"Carefully," Robbie replied, and Tony snickered. Then Robbie studied the perimeter of the crater. He spotted a slope that was not too steep to be treacherous. "Over there," he said, "past those boulders."

Tony cracked his knuckles. "All right, then. Let's go."

Robbie grabbed Tony's shoulder. "Not just yet. I think we need to wait until nightfall to get them."

"But that's hours away!" Jeff protested.

"Why do you want to wait until dark?" said Tony.

"They might see us coming in the daylight," Robbie pointed out. "And what if they brought a hunting rifle? We would never be able to get close enough to them then."

Tony saw the logic there. "Okay, good point. We'll wait until dark."

Robbie grinned. "They'll never see us coming."

CHAPTER 6

The sun went down a little after nine o'clock. Robbie and his cronies had made their way down the rocky ramp when there was still a little twilight in the sky, and now they were waiting on the sunken plateau's floor for it to get a little darker.

"Not much longer now," Robbie muttered. "Then we'll teach those assholes a lesson."

Jeff's excitement grew. "This is gonna be great. I can't wait to see the looks on their faces when we surprise them."

"We're gonna scare the hell out of 'em, that's for sure," added Tony.

That's not the half of it, thought Robbie. Dark thoughts swirled in his head. The things he wanted to do to those smug students brought him excitement and adrenaline.

A short while later, it was dark enough. Robbie felt that they could now approach the camp without being seen.

"All right," he said, pulling his switchblade from

his back pocket, "let's go."

The crew started walking toward the campsite. They stepped cautiously among the brush and leaf litter, not wanting to make any noise. They moved directly toward the campfire. It provided a more than ample beacon for them. As they got closer, they could see there were also two kerosene lanterns burning near the tents, providing light beyond the campfire's reach.

Robbie saw Betty Lou sitting contentedly by the fire. The sight of her enjoyment angered him even more. He also saw Tom and Chad tending to the campfire, using some of the many pieces of wood they had gathered earlier. Robbie led his group as close as he could, then stopped behind the tents. He waited a moment, reveling in the anticipation, before he surprised his victims.

"Lookie what we got here!" Robbie bellowed as he emerged.

The campers jumped, startled by the unexpected voice. They sprang to their feet and their heads whirled toward the visitor.

Robbie and his crew were but five feet away, all three of them smiling with terrifying delight. And all three had their switchblades out.

"Robbie!" said Tom, his hands halfway raised. "What are you doing here?"

"We came to finish our little chat from yesterday," Robbie replied.

Betty Lou's eyes were wide with fear. "No, please... just leave us alone!"

"No," said Robbie. "We have unfinished business." Looking at Betty Lou, he licked his upper lip. "Especially with you."

Tom's pulse was racing. "Look, Robbie, you're a smart guy. Think about it before you do something you'll regret. You know this can only end badly."

"Badly for you, maybe," said Tony. "Not us."

Chad tried to intervene. "Come on, fellas. My father—"

"I don't care that your old man is the sheriff!" Robbie snorted. "It won't do you a bit of good out here."

"What are you gonna do, then?" Chad said. "Keep us out here? Because you know my father's gonna hear about this otherwise."

"Not if he never finds the bodies," Robbie responded.

There was something in Robbie's voice that sent chills through the campers. Something that told them he was committed to doing something terrible.

"Please, Robbie," Tom reasoned. "If we've wronged you in any way, we're really sorry. Okay? We never meant to upset—"

A rustling in the distant trees was suddenly heard, subtle but noticeable.

"Who's that?" said Betty Lou, standing erect. "Did you bring someone else with you?"

Robbie's grin flattened. "No."

The others perked their ears to listen. They heard what sounded like a boulder quietly rolling through the nearby terrain.

"Who's out there?" Robbie called out.

Tom reached for one of the glass kerosene lanterns and held it high. Everybody tensed, scanning the trees that were illuminated by the lamp's light.

Betty Lou shrieked. Darting their eyes to where she was looking, the young men saw something unbelievable, horrifying.

An immense thing was slithering rapidly across the plateau, heading directly for the group of people. It was a snake, but unlike any that had been seen before. It was gigantic, as thick as an ox, with light gray scales the color of cement. The serpent was forty feet in length, with no eyes, and had a mouth large enough to swallow each of them whole.

"Shit!" Robbie yelped.

"Run!" said Tom.

Tom and his friends bolted away from the campground, and Robbie's crew decided to do the same. Jeff's legs tangled with Robbie's, however, and the three stumbled over each other. Robbie scampered over Jeff and ran. Tony hurried behind.

Jeff got up and faced the quick creature. He froze with fear. His body was numb; he could not control his muscles to move at all. He simply stared in awe of the horrifying thing coming toward him.

All Jeff saw was its pale skin and the enormous maw full of six-inch-long teeth. Then he was engulfed in darkness and he felt his body being pierced and crushed. Death came immediately.

The serpent continued its pursuit of human prey. It caught up to Tony next, who had never been a fast runner. With a little lunge, it was able to make contact with the fleeing human and knock him down. Tony fell forward and plowed against the rough ground. Adrenaline blocked the pain of his scraped face. Then he saw a mouth close upon him, followed by the intense force of jaws crushing him. He succumbed to death instantly.

There was more prey out there. The snake rushed on, going after the rest.

Robbie, who was not used to rigorous activity, was starting to feel his leg muscles burn. Fear kept him running, though, knowing he had no choice. He would get away, no matter how his muscles felt.

Suddenly, he tripped over something he couldn't see. It felt like a protruding tree root. Robbie tumbled forward, feeling grass and rocky ground meet him. A moment later, he regained his bearings and jumped to his feet.

It was too late.

Before he could resume running, he was taken by his pursuer. Powerful jaws clamped down around him, muffling his scream as they closed.

Tom and his friends were still running away. Tom looked back over his shoulder to see if the creature was still coming after them.

It sure was. And it was amazing how fast the huge snake was moving. It would be upon them in seconds.

"Quickly!" cried Tom, his wits kicking in. "Up a tree! Climb!"

The three students bolted desperately. They fled from the approaching monstrosity, wildly looking for a nearby tree to jump upon and climb. Tom grabbed Betty Lou's hand and yanked her to a large elm, boosting her high enough for her to take hold of the lower branches and pull herself up. Then he jumped for the branches to climb behind her. He grabbed one and walked up the trunk to aid his ascent to the branches.

Chad had run past the others, and the snake was locked in on him. Screaming in terror, he leaped onto a hardy trunk and scampered his way up its branches. His fingers gripped any knot or branch they could find to cling onto. Sheer adrenaline allowed him to ascend quickly, like a frightened monkey evading a lion. He looked down.

The gray creature below him paused for a moment, studying the thick oak tree with its snout. Sensing the heat of its prey above, it coiled around the base of the tree and lifted its immense head. Then it worked its way up the oak to capture its victim.

CHAPTER 7

Seeing the serpent coming after him, Chad's heart pounded frantically. He continued his climb through the treacherous branches, higher and higher, but the snake kept spiraling its way up behind him. In a matter of minutes, Chad could climb no further. The tight weave of branches would not allow him to continue his ascent.

Panicking, he looked around. One of the nearby trees was close, perhaps close enough to jump onto. But he was not sure he could make it. A glance down at the persistent creature, now just five feet below him with its terrible jaws opening, inspired him to take that chance.

Chad sprang from his perch, arms out, and he was met roughly by the branches of the neighboring tree. He groped for any hold his hands could secure. Fortunately, he caught enough of the tree to latch onto it and prevent his falling to the ground. He immediately looked over at the snake.

It was entangled in the branches of the oak tree, and seemed to have difficulty freeing itself. Chad wasted no time skinning down his tree. Upon reaching the ground, he called for his friends.

"Hey guys!" he informed. "I think it's stuck up the tree! What should we do?"

Tom, having watched his friend's antics, quickly had an idea. He dropped from the branches of his tree and ran to the campfire. Then, grabbing the glass lanterns, he rushed back to the trees. He loosened the fuel caps and hurled the lanterns up at the monster trapped in the tree.

The glass lanterns broke upon impact, the kerosene igniting instantly, brightly. The confined creature hissed and convulsed as it began to burn. But despite its frenetic efforts to escape the searing pain, it could not free itself from the branches of the oak. Now the tree was on fire as well. The fire quickly spread upward, engulfing the snake in a putrid, crackling blaze.

"Yes!" said Tom. "I think we got him!"

Covered in burning kerosene, the creature could do nothing to stop the intense pain. It writhed and spasmed violently. Its hissing was loud with fury and agony.

Betty Lou was mesmerized by the surreal sight. She still couldn't quite process the unbelievable thing that had happened. Her friends were just as awestruck. The youngsters watched unblinking until the monster was dead and sizzling.

"My God," slurred Chad. "What on Earth was

that?"

"I have no idea," Tom replied. "I've never heard of anything like that thing existing since the days of the dinosaurs." He continued staring upward at the giant serpent burning in the tree. "It must be some kind of prehistoric snake that has been awakened. My dad might know what it is."

Chad was still shaking. "I don't care *what* it is, as long as it's dead."

"Amen to that," Betty Lou seconded.

Tom nodded in agreement. The trio had just come dangerously close to death. It was a miracle that they had survived the attack.

"Are you all right?" said Tom, his eyes falling gently upon Betty Lou's.

"Yes, I think so," she replied. Then she took several deep, calming breaths.

He wrapped his arm around her and held her tightly. She nestled into the comfort of his chest.

"I should go and get my flashlight," Tom declared, "since the lanterns are gone now. We'll need the light."

"Good idea," said Chad.

Tom traipsed back to his tent to get his flashlight. He dug through his backpack until his fingers found it. Turning the light on, he promptly returned to his friends to finish watching the fire burn out.

Suddenly a distant rumbling was heard behind them.

Whirling with the flashlight and aiming it across the expanse, Tom scanned the ground around them. He saw nothing there. The moonlight enabled him to see movement on the cliffside. He saw rock separating and falling from the cliff wall above the large cave. Holding the light as steady as his shaking hands would allow, Tom studied the rocky cliff. Then something shook the rock again, and another wave of rubble tumbled to the ground. Rock was now breaking away below the cave as well.

"What the...?" Chad began, growing more fearful. Then he saw a gargantuan form writhing in the mouth of the cave, trying to force its way out. In the shaky light, he made out the image of another monstrous snake.

But this one was about ten times bigger than the first.

"Run!" Chad instinctively yelled.

The three campers wasted no time. Abandoning their camping gear and supplies, they bolted through the sunken area and headed straight for the earthslide ramp. Tom led them by the beam of his flashlight. They reached the steep slope and scampered up the earth and rubble.

They got to the top of the crater and took a moment to catch their breath. Their hearts were pounding. Tom looked over to the commotion around the cave, seeing the snout of something impossibly large trying to emerge.

"It's coming for us!" cried Betty Lou. "Just like the smaller one!"

"Let's get the hell out of here!" said Chad.

Tom aimed the flashlight down the wooded

hillside and started running down the long trail. The others followed him closely, desperate to escape the beast and get to the dormant Jeep at the bottom. They focused on each rapid step, careful not to do something like stumble and break an ankle. But they did need to run; every second counted.

Something broke through in the distance. Something that hissed so loud and strong that it almost sounded like an angry roar echoing through the dark hills. Then it came out of the crater and pushed its way down the hillside, cracking trees and sending them flying.

"Oh shit!" Chad blurted. "It's coming after us!"

Eyes wide with fear, the students ran for their lives. Their hearts were pounding and their minds were reeling. They couldn't believe what was happening. After what felt like an eternity, they could finally see the trailhead at the bottom.

Tom fumbled through his pocket for the keys while he was running. *Don't drop them*, he warned himself, *don't you dare drop them*. His shaking hands were focused and strong; he produced the keys and held them safely in his grip.

The three of them made it to the bottom, and the Jeep was in sight. They hurried to the vehicle and jumped inside. Tom fought to find the ignition in the dark.

Seeing the forest moving in front of them, Betty Lou screamed.

Tom's key found its home, and he started the Jeep. Then he ripped it into reverse, peeled away from the trailhead, and turned around to speed down the road.

"Oh my God," stammered Chad over the noise of the motor. "That thing we killed was nothing compared to what just came after us! I think we killed its baby!"

"If we did," Tom added, "then Mama's really ticked off!"

"Oh, we've got to find a telephone!" pleaded Betty Lou. "Stop at Frannie's, Tom! Please!"

"Yes," Tom nodded hastily. "We need to notify the authorities right away!"

CHAPTER 8

After a long stretch of dark, lonely road, they made their way to Frannie's Diner. Tom swerved the Jeep into the parking lot, skidding to a stop on the gravel. The three terrified students sprang from the vehicle and hurried inside to use the diner's telephone.

The smells of coffee, fried chicken, grilled hamburgers, and cigarettes greeted them when they entered. Their faces still pale with fright, they were quickly acknowledged by a waitress.

"What on Earth is eating you?" exclaimed Helen—the familiar, middle-aged waitress—when she encountered the frantic trio. "You kids look like you've seen a ghost!"

"A m-monster is more like it!" Tom stammered. "We need to use your telephone!"

The diner's patrons, hearing this, stopped eating and focused on the three visitors. All that could be heard was the record playing on the jukebox. Helen smiled reassuringly to her customers, then quietly led the students to the counter. She seated them on red leather stools and offered them the telephone from beneath the counter.

"Here you go, kids," she said softly.

"Thanks, Helen," said Tom.

"Relax," said Helen. "Can I get you all some water?"

The trio nodded thankfully.

Chad took the telephone and dialed the sheriff's station to reach his father.

The sheriff picked up on the other end. "Sheriff Burton here."

Thank God, thought Chad. "Dad, it's me! Listen, I know you're not gonna believe this, but there's a giant snake that attacked us when we were camping up by Little Mountain! And I mean *giant!* It's wider than a train, and probably a couple hundred feet long!"

The sheriff thought his son had gone crazy. "What? Look, son—"

"It's true! We couldn't believe it, either. And it killed Robbie Sullivan, and his pals Jeff and Tony!"

The sheriff started to speak on the other end, but then the line abruptly went dead.

"Hello? *Hello?*" begged Chad. But the connection was gone. Numb, he turned to his friends. "The telephone line's down," he said helplessly.

"That's not good," Tom murmured.

Suddenly, the ceiling of the diner caved in at the far corner. A handful of patrons disappeared in a blur of drywall, lumber, and dust. Everyone else jumped and shrieked, their eyes quickly darting to the source of the cacophony. As the dust cloud cleared, their faces grew white from what they saw.

A monstrous head was moving atop the rubble, as large as a bus. It was the gigantic snake.

Helen and her customers screamed and ran wildly for the exit. Hearing the screams, the eyeless creature thrust its gray head deeper into the diner. It opened its sticky mouth wide, showing long, narrow teeth. Locking in on the heat of its prey, it devoured several people with one closing of its mammoth jaw.

"This way!" yelled Helen, heading for the kitchen. Tom and Chad reacted at once, pulling Betty Lou with them. The three followed Helen into the kitchen and behind the grills.

"What's going on out there?" the head cook shouted.

"A-A monster!" Helen informed him. "My lord, Pete, it's a giant *monster!*"

"It followed us!" cried Betty Lou, her chest heaving with panic. "Oh my God, it's still after us!"

Chad was mortified. "How did it find us?"

"It's as if it has learned our scents!" Tom exclaimed.

The thought sent shudders through the trio.

The creature started burrowing through the wall around the kitchen doors.

Pete screamed and quickly grabbed a stock pot of boiling water. He doused the snake's snout with its contents, and the beast recoiled slightly. But then it lunged forward, crushing the cook's body into the steel door of the walk-in freezer.

While the serpent was focused on the cook, Helen yanked the others through a short hallway and to the back door. The four of them rushed out into the night air. Then they crept around the corner of the building to get to the parking lot.

The serpent was halfway into the diner now, its enormous tail whipping down forcefully on the ground outside. Several cars were smashed in the parking lot, but fortunately Tom's Jeep was unharmed. Shaking, Tom pulled his keys from his pocket and led the group around the tail end of the monster.

Running along the perimeter of the parking lot, Betty Lou's heart was pounding rapidly. She feared that the creature would pull its head out of the diner and notice them. Each second that she ran, she was terrified that the monster would do just that.

Don't let it catch us, don't let it catch us, she prayed. *I don't want to be eaten alive!*

The group quickly made it to the Jeep. Leaping inside, they held on as Tom started the motor. He floored the gas pedal and sped away while the creature was busy tearing up the inside of Frannie's Diner.

CHAPTER 9

Half an hour later, the Jeep arrived in town. Tom veered to the curb in front of the police station, his brakes squealing the vehicle to an abrupt stop. The four then scurried inside the station to report what had happened.

"Sheriff!" hailed Tom. "We called you from Frannie's, but the snake must've knocked down the telephone poles!"

Sheriff Burton rose from his chair, his stout belly barely clearing the desk. "Now, now, just hold on a minute. What are you talking about, Tom? I heard the same craziness from my son earlier," he said, pointing a finger at Chad.

"Look, you're gonna think I'm pulling your leg, but I swear it's all true. My friends here will corroborate."

"And what's this about people being killed?"

"Robbie Sullivan and his buddies, Jeff and Tony. They came up to where we were camping to attack us, but luckily for us the snake got to them before they could hurt us."

The sheriff didn't know what to make of this. "Okay, just tell me everything that happened."

Tom drew a deep breath. "Okay, we were camping up by Little Mountain and we saw a large area that had recently collapsed a hundred feet below ground level."

"What?"

"You know, like a sinkhole. But hundreds of yards across. We went down to check it out, and after we set up camp, Robbie and his pals snuck up on us and said they were going to make us disappear. While we were trying to talk sense into them, we saw a huge snake coming for us! It chased us all, getting to Robbie's gang first. It... ate them. Then it followed us up a tree and got stuck. We got down from the tree and burned it. We were lucky enough to kill it, but then its mama came out of the ground after us! And it's gigantic! I swear, it must be a relative of the dinosaurs or something!"

The sheriff folded his arms, smirking under his mustache. "What? I've a good mind to call your father, Tom."

"Please do, sir," Tom said politely. "He needs to know about this. In fact, the whole *town* does!"

"Now look here—"

"It's true, Sheriff!" said Helen, still shaking. "It's a giant snake! It destroyed the diner, and ate a bunch of people! You're gonna need to call in the National Guard!"

Still skeptical, but sensing that he needed to

investigate, the sheriff stepped to the dispatch radio. He pressed the transmit button and spoke. "This is Sheriff Burton. Are there any units in the vicinity of Frannie's Diner?"

The voice of Deputy Sommers crackled through the speaker. "Yeah, Sheriff, this is Larry. I'm heading out that way right now to check on them. Seems their telephones don't work, so I want to make sure they didn't lose power as well. I've just left town."

"Okay, good. This may be nothing, but I've got a couple of—"

The sheriff was interrupted by the deputy's suddenly-horrified voice. "Oh my God! Oh my God! There's a monster coming this way! It's—it's a *snake!* A giant, monster snake! Lord, lord—" The words were cut off by the sounds of glass and metal being wrecked, which was quickly followed by the silence of the deputy's radio transmitter being released.

Everybody in the police station was stunned, motionless. After a moment of shock, urgency snapped Tom's thoughts to the problem at hand. "He said he was just leaving town. That means the thing has almost reached town! We've got to warn everybody!"

The sheriff grabbed his radio and ushered the group outside. He started his police cruiser and pulled away from the station. Tom and the others followed in the Jeep. They sped toward the edge of town in an attempt to save as many townspeople as possible.

CHAPTER 10

It only took a few minutes to reach the edge of town. But they were too late; the beast was already there. It had punched its way through the living room wall of a house, catching its unsuspecting meal inside. One of the inhabitants was bitten in half, and her legs fell to the ground and twitched.

Sheriff Burton was momentarily frozen, trying to process what the headlights were showing him. He could not believe he was actually seeing the giant monster that was before him, its ashy gray head looming above the broken house. The head alone looked like it weighed several tons. Then the creature turned to the house next door, smashed down on it, and dug through the rubble for its next victims.

The sheriff snapped out of his daze and flipped on his siren to bring the neighbors to their windows. Following suit, Tom began palming the Jeep's horn. Sure enough, the neighbors came to their windows to see what the commotion was.

The serpent heard the painful sound of the siren,

and it was angered. It pulled out of the house, removing large sections of siding and roofing that then fell to the lawn. Turning its monstrous head, it opened its mouth and made for the police cruiser.

The sheriff stepped on the gas and turned to evade the behemoth. What was he to do now? It was obvious that the townspeople were not safe inside their homes. But where was the safest, most fortified structure in town? Then it came to him. While driving along the street, he activated his loudspeaker.

"Everybody evacuate! Everybody evacuate! Run into town, get to the church! I repeat, get to the church!"

Tom was driving right behind the sheriff, staying close. The snake had now honed in on Tom's Jeep and veered toward it. Betty Lou, her head turned back to see the nightmarish creature coming for them, screamed hysterically. Tom downshifted and floored the gas pedal.

In an attempt to lure the monster away from the houses, Tom whipped the Jeep down a side street. The serpent followed, ignoring the police car. While Tom revved away, the residents fled their homes and jumped into their cars to follow the sheriff.

Sheriff Burton reached for his radio and pressed the call button on the microphone. "Deputy Johnson! Come in!"

The sheriff's other deputy, Terry Johnson, answered. "Johnson here, over."

"Terry, we've got a crisis. There is a giant snake running around, and it's busting through houses to eat the people inside."

"Wh-wh—"

"I know, I thought it was crazy too. Until I saw it with my own eyes."

"Okay…"

"And Larry's dead. The monster got him before it came into town."

"Jesus," the deputy said quietly. "What do we do?"

"I'm bringing as many people as I can to the church. It's a strong structure, and I think we'll be safe inside there. Meet us there."

"Ten-four."

***

Tom weaved wildly through the streets in an attempt to elude the beast. He drove past Main Street and headed for the commercial part of town, hoping to keep the monster away from residential areas. The beast was in relentless pursuit.

Tom's heart was pounding mercilessly. The giant serpent was slithering fast, rumbling over parked cars and gaining ground on the hapless Jeep. Tom knew they could be overtaken if the creature was to lunge at the right moment.

He wrenched the wheel to the left, skidding toward a lifeless warehouse. The passengers were jarred, but maintained their grips on the Jeep to stay on board. "Hang on!" exclaimed Tom. He steered the Jeep through the locked glass entryway doors. The vehicle smashed its way inside, past the reception area, and through the drywall into the expanse of the empty warehouse.

The giant serpent slowed to alter its course. Then it plunged its ashen head into the hole made by the Jeep. Within moments it locked in on the Jeep again. Lunging, the beast propelled its long body toward its prey.

Tom whipped the Jeep to the right, and the serpent went skidding past. Eyes wide with panic, he circled back to the front entryway. The snake's tail had just been pulled inside, out of the way, and Tom was fortunate enough to guide the Jeep back outside into the night.

The snake convulsed inside, trying to turn around. The structure was too confining. Pushing and flexing, the beast managed to tear the warehouse apart from roof to walls. By the time it had leveled the building to break free, the Jeep it sought was gone.

CHAPTER 11

Tom brought the Jeep to the old church in town. A multitude of cars were already there, the citizens having followed the sheriff to the sturdy building. A hearty stone structure, it would provide the best protection in town. Tom and Chad leaped out of the Jeep, and Betty Lou and Helen came down from the back seat. The group hustled inside to join the rest of the townspeople.

Betty Lou quickly spotted her parents in the nave. A wave of relief washed through her, and she ran to them to seek comfort.

"Glad you made it, son," said the sheriff, pleased to see Chad and his friends.

Tom scanned the room inside. His father was not among the others. "Where's my dad?"

Sheriff Burton looked around as well, confirming that Hank was not there. "He must be at home."

"I've got to go get him!" Tom said urgently.

The sheriff was not keen on letting one of his

son's friends go back out there where it was dangerous. "No, Tom, you stay here with us. We'll collect him." The sheriff addressed Deputy Johnson. "Terry, drive over to the Defray residence and get Hank, will you?"

"Yes, sir," said the deputy. He grabbed his keys and walked briskly out of the church.

"Don't worry, Tom," the sheriff assured, "we'll get your father here safely."

"Okay," said Tom. "Thanks."

"Now come on, let's gather with the others."

They went to the middle of the church and joined the townspeople who had made it there. There were a lot of frightened faces massed together, some of the folk holding each other for comfort. Tom, standing behind Betty Lou, saw that and it prompted him to wrap his arms around Betty Lou's shoulders.

"Oh, Tom," she said, "I can't believe what's happening. It's like a nightmare that I can't wake up from."

"I know," Tom replied. "But we have to keep hope."

She turned around to face him. "Hope? Against a monster like that?" The panic in her eyes made Tom feel helpless.

Chad looked at his father with that same panic in his eyes. "What are we going to do now, Dad?"

"I radioed the state police on the way here," Deputy Johnson reported. "They should be arriving soon to help us."

"That's a relief," breathed Tom. "We need all the

help we can get. We may even need the National Guard to fight this monster!"

"It's all our fault!" blurted the town priest, Father Flanagan. "We've been tearing up our planet without thinking there would be consequences." Turning to Tom, he continued. "The sheriff told us what you kids said to him. The sunken area, where you found the monster, was undoubtedly a result of overmining. Our greed was bound to stir up the balance of nature. We pillage God's creation, and now this beast has come to punish us. It is Hell's serpent!"

Sheriff Burton, sensing the helpless dread building inside the listening townspeople, began to interject. "Listen, it's just an animal. I know humans have been taking advantage of the Earth and its resources, but that doesn't mean there's some biblical retribution…"

A loud concussion was heard from the wall, its vibration felt across the floor by all. The church's lights went out a second later. Amid the panicked screams of the crowd, the sheriff kept cool. He pulled out his flashlight and turned it on to illuminate the room.

"It's the snake!" Betty Lou exclaimed. "It's found us!"

Father Flanagan knew what to do. "Quick, everybody! To the basement!" He led the terrified group down a set of stairs behind the pulpit. The townsfolk scurried down the staircase, and the priest shut the basement door behind them. And just in time. Above them, the serpent smashed through the stone wall and landed its head heavily on the now-vacant floor. After a moment of analysis, the beast hammered on the timbers of the church floor.

"I thought we lost it!" whined Helen, being showered with dust and splinters. "How does it know we're down here? It's like it has ESP!"

"Of course!" exclaimed Tom. "It's following the *heat* of the people! The snake lives deep in the Earth's crust, where there's no light. That explains why it has no eyes; it's subterranean and it hunts by sensing sound and heat. It'll be able to find us no matter where we go."

"So we should've split up and spread out?" asked Betty Lou fearfully.

Another blow to the floor above, and some of the timbers cracked.

Tom suddenly had an ambitious idea. "Or keep staying together," he said.

All eyes turned to him with confusion.

"I think I have an idea," he explained. "What if we could get it to follow us some place where we can kill it? I don't know, maybe to the power plant to electrocute it or something."

Chad's face lit up with hope. "Tom, that's a brilliant idea!" Then he addressed his father. "Do you think there's some way to make that work?"

The sheriff processed the idea for a moment, remembering his days working at the power station, then nodded. "Yes, I think that's possible. Let's make a run for it through the side cellar door, and everybody meet up at the power plant outside town on Hill Road. On the way, I'll make a call to the plant and have them set up for us."

All were in agreement; they knew they would not last much longer if they stayed in the bowels of the church. As a bunched group, they all pushed through the cellar door and spilled out onto the church grounds. From there they filed into their cars and hurried east toward Hill Road.

The serpent abandoned its demolition of the church, turned its head east, and chased after its prey.

CHAPTER 12

Deputy Johnson arrived at Hank Defray's house and skidded to a stop. He trotted to the porch and knocked on the front door. A minute later, the herpetologist opened the door.

"Hello, Deputy," said Hank. "What can I do for you?"

"Listen, Hank, there's not a lot of time to explain. But we're dealing with a town emergency, and I've been told to collect you and see that you're safe."

Hank frowned. "Town emergency? What's happened?"

"I'll tell you in the car. Please, Hank!"

The scientist noted the sincere panic in the deputy's voice, as well as in his eyes. "All right, all right. Let's go."

Hank closed the house up and followed the deputy to his cruiser. He got in on the passenger side while Deputy Johnson hopped into the driver's seat and put the car in gear. Then Hank was rushed away down the street.

"What's this all about?" asked Hank. "Where are we going?"

"Listen, we're going to the church," the deputy informed. "There's a giant—well, *snake*—tearing up the town, and that's the safest place to be."

"I'm sorry, did you say—"

"Yes, Hank. Giant snake!" Deputy Johnson had to chuckle. "Something right up your alley, now that I think about it."

"How big is this snake?"

"You'd have to see it to believe it. It's as big as a train!"

Hank didn't believe a word of that. Surely the policeman was having a joke at the snake scientist's expense. "Come on now," Hank said drearily.

"Okay, I'll show you what it did," said the deputy.

He drove the police car to the neighborhood the serpent had been through. When Hank saw the crushed houses and cars, his mouth fell open. The damage left in the creature's wake was unimaginable.

"Oh my God," he muttered. "You weren't lying." He was mesmerized by the destruction they were riding past.

"See? This monster is smashing people, cars, and even houses! Left and right! Your son was concerned for your safety while this thing is rampaging, so that's why the sheriff had me come get you."

The mention of Tom, who was supposed to be out camping, snapped his attention back to the deputy. "Where is my son?"

"He's at the church already, waiting for me to come back with you. He's the one who warned us about the monster."

Sheriff Burton's voice suddenly crackled on the radio. "Terry, are you out there?"

Deputy Johnson picked up the mouthpiece. "I'm here, Sheriff. And I have Hank Defray with me."

"Good. Listen, don't go to the church! The snake destroyed it. Now it's chasing us through town!"

Hank was concerned for the safety of his son. "Tom…" he uttered helplessly.

The deputy wasn't sure how to reply to the update. "Well, what should I do with Hank and myself?"

"Come to the power station; that's where we're all gathering!"

"The power station? Why in the world—"

"Just do it!" said the sheriff. "We're hoping to lure it there so we can try to kill it with electricity!"

"Ten-four," said Deputy Johnson. "We're on our way."

Hank gripped the upholstery of the seat, anxious to get to his son, while the deputy sped away.

CHAPTER 13

The creature came fast and angry. It locked in on the heat of the fleeing cars, moving its thunderous body muscles expeditiously to speed after them through the heart of town. The snake bounced between buildings while moving, cracking brick and shattering glass. Several of the smaller buildings collapsed from the impact of the behemoth, and many parked cars were crushed by its scaly girth. The thickness of the subterranean creature's scales prevented it from any injury.

The caravan of vehicles sped through town. The drivers ran stoplights and hopped sidewalk corners to keep ahead of their pursuer. By the time they reached the eastern edge of town, they had gained a little distance between themselves and the creature.

Not slowing down, the sheriff turned on Hill Road and continued to lead the group toward the power station.

"We can't lose it!" said Chad.

"I know," the sheriff replied. "It will find us no

matter where we go. But if we can just get to the power station in time to be ready for it, we might survive."

A few miles up the road, the sheriff's procession was met by a welcome sight: five black state police cruisers speeding their way with rotating lights flashing.

"Thank God," he said, turning to his passengers. "Help has arrived."

The sheriff stopped just long enough to speak to the driver of the lead vehicle. "I'm Sheriff Burton. The thing's coming behind us, and it's huge! We're heading to the power plant to lure it there and try to kill it with electricity! But we need to buy some time to get everything ready there!"

The officer nodded from behind his rolled-down window. "Get your people out there, Sheriff, and we'll stay here and try to take it down with mass firepower."

The sheriff nodded and sped along, the townspeople's cars following.

The state troopers parked beside each other, forming a line of defense. The captain stepped out of the lead vehicle, waving for the attention of the others.

"All right, boys, this is it! I don't quite know what to expect, but if the sheriff is right, we're in for a fight! Grab everything you've got, and get ready to fire!"

Though skeptical, the troopers obeyed. They went to the trunks of their vehicles and pulled out their shotguns, semi-automatic M1 carbine rifles, and submachine guns.

"I'm still betting this is all a practical joke," said

one of the troopers.

"Yeah," snorted another. "I wouldn't be surprised if the captain himself is behind this. Some sort of practice drill, maybe?"

"Gotta be. There's no way a monster like that could possibly exist."

Their doubts were soon obliterated minutes later when they saw the monster coming at them in the dark distance. The sight sucked the breath from their lungs. Adrenaline surging, the men sighted their weapons and aimed.

The cynical trooper was now holding his M1 with shaking hands. "Oh Jesus, oh Jesus…"

"Okay, men!" the captain barked. "On my order…"

The shape in the night became more detailed as it neared. It was like something out of Hell. A nightmare like no other. The troopers heard the ground rumble beneath the monster as it crawled steadily toward them.

"…*Fire!*"

Bursts of semi-automatic gunfire rattled the beast. Feeling the barrage of bullets striking its scaled body, it recoiled.

"Hit it with everything we've got!" ordered the captain.

Shotgun blasts, .30 rifle fire, and .45 Tommy gun rounds continued to hit home. But all of the rounds fired could not drop the creature. It retaliated by swinging its head down to crush its enemies.

"Look out!"

The troopers in its path leaped out of the way just before the giant head slammed into the ground. They quickly regrouped and continued their firing.

Deputy Johnson's speeding cruiser arrived at the scene. The sight of the gigantic creature doing battle with armed forces made Hank's heart skip a beat.

"Jesus!" he blurted. "Look at that beast!" He couldn't take his eyes off the fascinating specimen.

The deputy did not slow down. "Let's get around it while it's busy fighting!"

The cruiser veered off the road, rumbling over the bumpy ground. Keeping a wide berth around the creature and its active tail, Deputy Johnson navigated the landscape to get past the beast. Then he steered back onto the road and continued toward the power station.

The gunfire continued to crack through the night air. The bullets struck the creature, but did not seem to penetrate.

The giant serpent again reacted violently. It swooped its head down upon the enemy, flattening one of the cruisers. A handful of state police that were too close died instantly.

Then the beast swung its massive head side to side, whipping some of the other cruisers away into the night like plastic toys.

The fight was hopeless. "Let's get out of here!" cried the captain.

The remaining troopers scrambled to the vehicles that were still intact. They pulled into gear and took off. The serpent took one of the cruisers, crushing the car and its occupants in its jaws. The rest of the vehicles retreated up Hill Road.

CHAPTER 14

Deputy Johnson's cruiser skidded to a halt on the gravel at the power station. He jumped out of the car and over to Hank's side, but Hank had already exited the vehicle as well. Spotting the group of people behind the chain-link fence, they hurried over to join them.

"Dad!" said Tom, seeing his father arrive. "I'm glad to see you."

"Same about you," said the herpetologist. He wrapped his arm over Tom's shoulder. "I had to be with you while you're out here with this thing. I'm glad you're okay."

"For now, at least."

"Can you believe this, Hank?" the waitress Helen shuddered. "It's like a nightmare and we can't wake up!"

"I think it's sensing our heat or smelling our scent in order to track us down," said Tom. "And it's not giving up."

"I know," Hank nodded. "We passed it on the way

here while the troopers were fighting it. It's incredible."

"It's a real monster," Chad added. "Like something out of prehistoric times. Like a giant dinosaur."

"What do you think, Hank?" the sheriff asked. "Do you think it's prehistoric?"

"It would stand to reason," said Hank. "But the largest prehistoric snake we've found so far was the *Gigantophis garstini*, but even that only grew to a length of thirty to thirty-five feet. And besides, they were found on the other side of the world. Of the prehistoric snakes found in *this* region, dating from the Pennsylvanian to Quaternary periods, the largest were only about twenty feet long. What we've seen tonight is like nothing ever heard of. This thing must be twenty feet wide and a couple hundred feet long."

Just then, the defeated state troopers reached the power station. They abandoned their cruisers next to the mass of cars along the road and ran to the power station's gate. The chain-link fence was opened to bring them in.

"Is that all of you?" asked Sheriff Burton.

The captain nodded. "All that's left," he panted. "That damn thing is unstoppable! Where the hell did something like that come from?"

"I think you just answered your own question," said Father Flanagan. "It came from Hell."

"Never mind that, sir," Tom interjected. "All that matters now is whether or not we can kill it. Our only hope is to stay here together, attracting it to us with our body heat, and hope it can be killed by electricity."

"Sounds like that's our only remaining option," nodded the captain. "We all need to pray."

A grinding rumble was heard in the distance, like a giant granite roller moving earth before it.

Dread fell over Betty Lou. *Oh God, it's coming.*

Hearts pounding, the townspeople gazed into the night awaiting their inevitable hunter. The behemoth was soon visible in the light of the power station.

"Get ready!" the sheriff directed. "Everybody stand back over there, behind the transformers!" The townspeople shrank back against the power station's front wall.

The serpent felt their heat; it was strong, aided by the energy of their pounding hearts. It lured the beast directly to their location. The snake reared its head forty feet up into the air, emitting a resounding hiss of triumph.

The crowd cowered in fear, hoping beyond all hope that their plan would work. They watched, frozen, as the monster came down across the chain-link fence. When its two-ton head pressed against the row of transformers, there was a blinding white flash.

200,000 volts instantly passed through its scales and into the serpent, coursing through its enormous body. The snake's muscles locked, making it helpless to withdraw. Within moments the body began to cook, sending a malicious odor into the air. Its smell made Father Flanagan think of fire and brimstone. Then the beast stopped convulsing.

It was dead.

CHAPTER 15

The following morning, Tom and Chad led the sheriff and the state police to where the monster came from. It was much easier to find than before; all they had to do was follow the path of leveled trees up the hillside. Hank went with the group, as the sheriff thought it wise to have the snake expert with them.

The small army arrived at the top of the crater to see the devastated landscape. The emergence of the giant serpent had damaged the forest life and spread rock all around the enormous hole it had made.

"My lord," said Hank. "It's unbelievable."

"That's where it came from," Chad said, unnecessarily pointing.

"We have to seal it up," the state police captain stated. "Just in case there are any more of them."

"Or their babies," added Tom.

The trooper nodded. "All right, let's find a way down there."

"We got down from over there," Tom said, pointing to the earthslide ramp he and his friends had used.

The cavalcade followed Tom to the earthen slope and carefully down into the sunken crater. From there, they moved directly to the hole at the rock wall. They stared into the mouth of the expanse, weapons drawn, to make sure nothing was coming from within to meet them.

Nothing did; the coast was clear.

"Okay boys," said Sheriff Burton, "let's blast it."

The troopers wasted no time setting explosives. With dynamite bundles and a spool of detonating cord, they laced the perimeter with destructive force.

"All right, everyone," the captain yelled, "take cover!"

Everybody moved away from the cave and across the ground until there was no more cord left. The captain attached the cord to the detonator while the others took cover behind the trees.

"Here we go!" The captain pushed the detonator handle down.

Covering their ears, the group watched while the explosives detonated with deafening, ground-shaking blasts. Granite was blown apart violently, falling heavy into the expanse to seal the entrance. When the dust finally settled, the hole was sealed with rock.

Satisfied with their work, the state troopers congratulated each other and made their way out of the crater.

If there were any more of the monstrous serpents, Tom could only pray that they would not find another way out.

THE END

AUTHOR'S NOTE

This tale, an homage to the giant-monster movies of the '50s and '60s, was birthed from one of my short stories written in 2013, titled *The Devil's Serpent*, which is one of the stories now residing in my book *Fragments And Shards*. I like the story so much that I decided I needed to develop it into a novella. Thank you for checking it out, and I truly hope you enjoyed it! As always, take care of yourselves, love your loved ones, and may life bless you with as many days as it can.

ABOUT THE AUTHOR

Michael Yowell was born in Colorado, where he grew up loving horror in various forms—comics, movies, and ultimately books. He began writing short stories, some of which have now been published in various anthologies and ezines, as well as in his own books *Fragments And Shards* and *Fragments And Shards II*. His other novels include *Devilhouse, The Camera Eye, The Dogcatcher, The Dogcatcher II: Chupacabras, The Dogcatcher III: Werewolf Queen, Sliggers, Sligger Island, Sligger Invasion, Ghostfield, Pirantulas, A Touch Of Death, The Mine,* and his Western *Red Pines*. He now resides in South Carolina with his wife Vanessa, where he continues to write his dreams and nightmares. He can be reached at michaelyowellhorror@gmail.com.

Check out other great

Dinosaur Thrillers!

Julian Michael Carver

TRIASSIC

After spending many years in artificial hypersleep, a handful of survivors of the exploration vessel Supernova awaken to find their ship torn to shreds. They are unsure of what happened in space or how they crashed into an uncharted planet. Upon exploration of the new world, they soon realize their destination: The Triassic, the first chapter of the Mesozoic Era. A plan is formulated to escape this terrifying landscape plagued with dinosaurs and prehistoric beasts. The survivors soon discover that there may be an even larger threat looming under the trees than just the dinosaurs, threatening to cut their mission short and trap them all forever in the primitive depths of the Triassic.

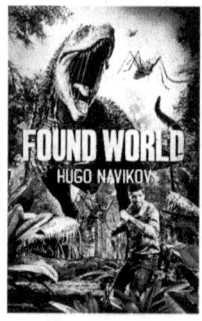

Hugo Navikov

THE FOUND WORLD

A powerful global cabal wants adventurer Brett Russell to retrieve a superweapon stolen by the scientist who built it. To entice him to travel underneath one of the most dangerous volcanoes on Earth to find the scientist, this shadowy organization will pay him the only thing he cares about: information that will allow him to avenge his family's murder. But before he can get paid, he and his team must enter an underground hellscape of killer plants, giant insects, terrifying dinosaurs, and an army of other predators never previously seen by man. At the end of this journey awaits a revelation that could alter the fate of mankind ... if they can make it back from this horrifying found world.

Check out other great

Dinosaur Thrillers!

Steve Metcalf

OBJEKT 221

Ruthless multi-national conglomerate Allied Genetics is under siege from a paramilitary force for hire. Allied calls in reinforcements and fortifies their crown-jewel property – an abandoned Soviet military facility in Crimea known during the Cold War as Objekt 221. Fortunately for the future of their research, O221 straddles a stretch of rocky landscape that hides a rift – a portal through time and space. Through this rift, Allied Genetics can travel, at will, to the Cretaceous – 100 million years into Earth's past – and bolster their genetic experiments with dinosaur DNA ... something their competitors want to stop at all costs."Objekt 221" is a story blending numerous science fiction elements such as repurposed military facilities, time travel, rogue corporate armies, dinosaurs and the hint of a super-ancient civilization.

Bestselling collection

PREHISTORIC:
A DINOSAUR ANTHOLOGY

PREHISTORIC is an action packed collection of stories featuring terrifying creatures that once ruled the Earth. Lost worlds where T-Rex and Velociraptors still roam and man is now on the menu. Laboratories at the forefront of cloning technology experiment with dinosaurs they do not understand or are able to contain. The deepest parts of the ocean where Megalodon, the largest and most ferocious predator to have ever existed is stalking new prey. Plus many more thrillers filled with extinct prehistoric monsters written by some of the best creature feature authors this side of the Jurassic period.

SEVEREDPRESS

🐦 @severedpress
f /severedpress

Check out other great
Dinosaur Thrillers!

Rick Poldark
PRIMORDIAL ISLAND

During a violent storm Flight 207 crash-lands in the South China Sea. Poseidon Tech tracks the wreckage to an uncharted island and dispatches a curious salvage team—two paleontologists, a biologist specializing in animal behavior, a botanist, and a nefarious big game hunter. Escorted by a heavily-armed security team, they cut through the jungle and quickly find themselves in a terrifying fight for survival, running a deadly gauntlet of prehistoric predators. In their quest for the flight recorder, they uncover the mystery of the island's existence and discover an arcane force that will tip the balance of power on the primordial island. Things are not as they seem as they race against time to survive the island's man-eating dinosaurs and make it back home in one piece.

P.K. Hawkins
SUBTERRANEA

Fall, 1985. The small town of Kettle Hollow barely shows up on any maps, and four young friends are used to taking their BMX's outside of town in an effort to find anything interesting to do. But tonight their tendency to go off by themselves may have saved them, and also forced them into the adventure of a lifetime.While they were away, Kettle Hollow has been locked down by the government, and a portal to another world has opened on Main Street. It's a world deep below the ground, a world where dinosaurs roam free, where giant plants and mutant insects hunt for prey. It's also a world where all their family and friends have been kidnapped for sinister purposes. Now, with time running out before the portal closes, the four friends must brave the unknown to save their loved ones. Time is running out, and in the darkened tunnels of Subterranea, something is hunting them.